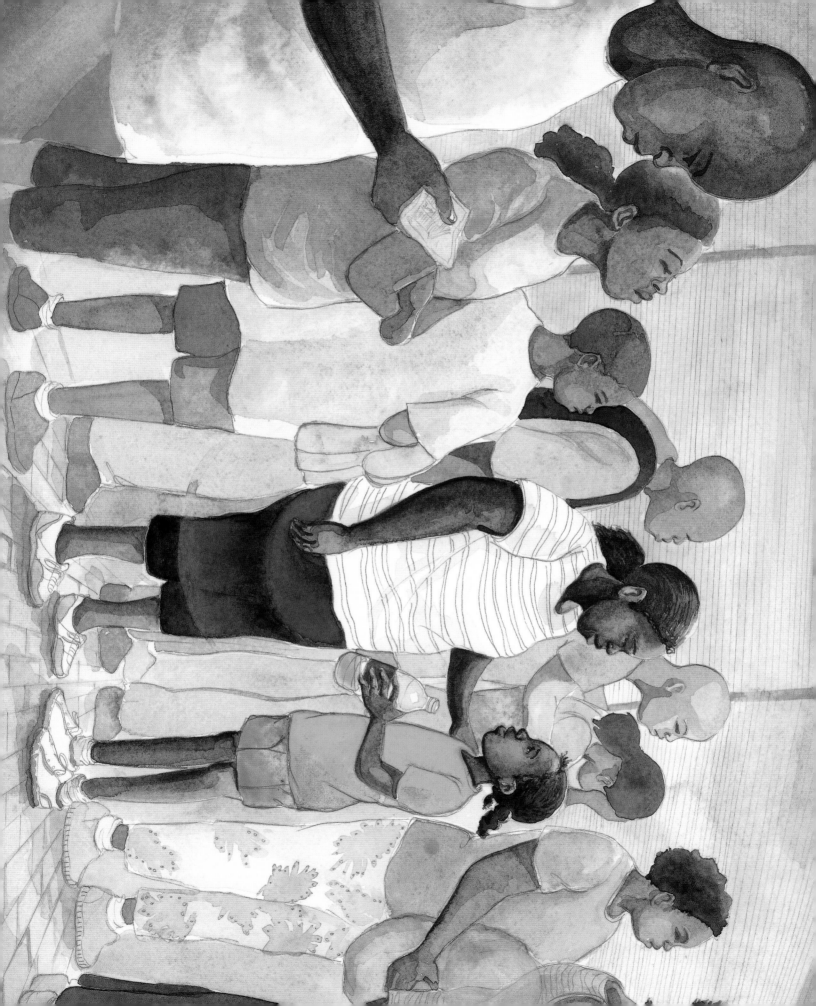

Keesha

I'm waiting in line at the Superdome
for the buses to come to take us to a safe place.
My family has been waiting for five days.
Finally, the buses are here. The line is long.
I can't see where it begins or ends.
I'm thirsty, but there's no water to drink.
The woman next to my family lives in the same parish,
but we've never met before.
She shares her water with me.
I open the bottle and drink as fast as I can,
but Momma tells me to slow down, save some for later.
I thank the woman.
I think maybe I'll send her one of my teddy bears
when we get back home.

Michael

A rescue team came and saved my family.
They took us to a shelter.
Today, we're home for the first time in six months.
We're moving into a trailer.
Things aren't what they used to be.
The houses on our block are damaged bad.
Things aren't what they used to be.
My tree is the only tree on the block still standing.
Things aren't what they used to be.
Katrina turned New Orleans inside out.
She crumbled roofs, blew away houses
and put everything that was *inside* out on the street.
Things aren't what they used to be.

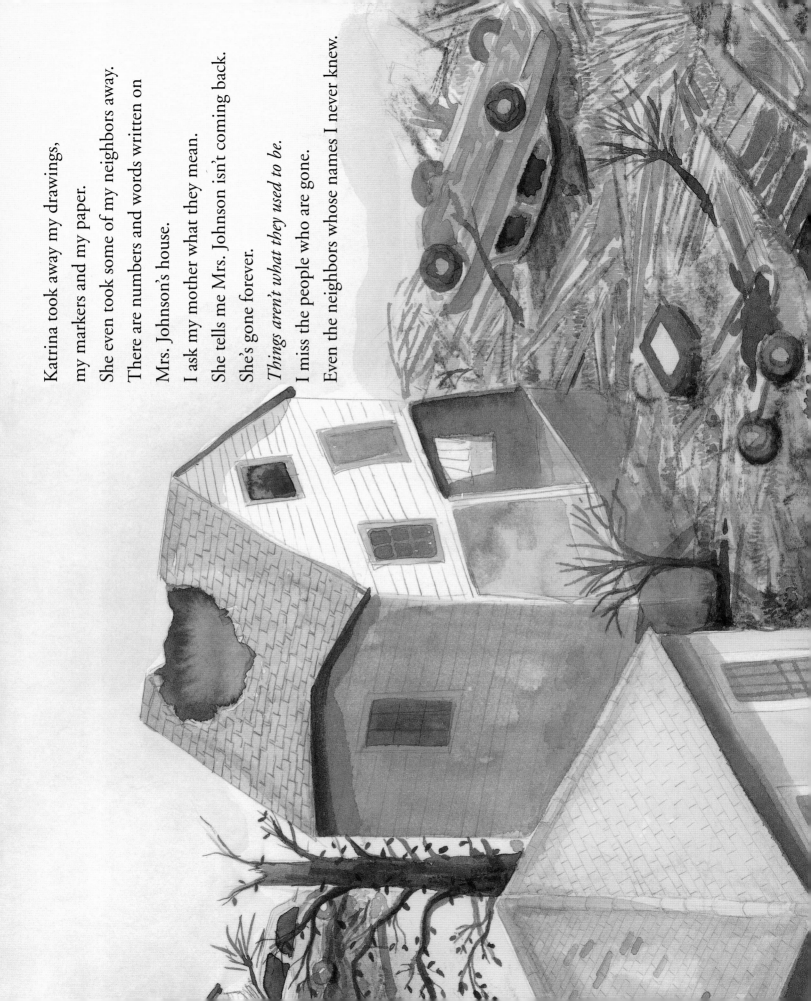

Katrina took away my drawings,
my markers and my paper.
She even took some of my neighbors away.
There are numbers and words written on
Mrs. Johnson's house.
I ask my mother what they mean.
She tells me Mrs. Johnson isn't coming back.
She's gone forever.
Things aren't what they used to be.
I miss the people who are gone.
Even the neighbors whose names I never knew.

Tommy

My father says not to complain.
He says not to pout when I don't get my way.
He tells me to stop thinkin' 'bout what I don't have.
He says I have more than others
and to be thankful for that.
But it's hard to be thankful.
Livin' in Houston isn't fun at all.
I am sleepin' on the floor
'cause the house is so crowded.
And I have to share everything.
I don't understand why my dad says
some got it worse.
But then he turns on the TV
and we watch the news.
I think of Adrienne, Michael and Keesha
and I hope they are not the ones
my dad is talkin' 'bout.

Keesha

Dear Adrienne,

We're staying in a trailer outside our broken house.

Katrina took my teddy bears away. I don't have any.

I play outside with Michael, but it's not the same without you and Tommy.

Adrienne, don't forget about me, hear?

I'm still your best friend.

The only friend that can twirl the rope at the perfect speed so you don't trip.

Don't forget how I keep the night-light on for you when you spend the night.

Don't forget how good I can dance and how I show you how to move too.

We can still be best friends, right?

Even though we're not living on the same block.

Adrienne, don't forget about me, hear?

Don't forget I'm still your best friend.

　　　　Love,

　　　　Keesha

Adrienne

Dear Keesha,

Granny told me the best news today.
Our house is fixed and we're coming back home.
Keesha, I didn't forget any of you.
I remember how Tommy likes baseball
and how Michael loves to draw.
And I didn't forget how much you like teddy bears.

Love,
Adrienne

Tommy

We're goin' back to New Orleans.
Got family and friends to see.
We're goin' to the French Quarter,
eat a snowball and some beignets.
We're goin' to listen to the street bands
playin' on the corner.
We're goin' back home.
No traffic jam today.
We'll be there in no time.

Michael

Adrienne and her granny are back.
They brought gifts for all of us.
They give Keesha a white teddy bear
and Tommy a baseball.
But I get the best gift of all—
a sketchbook and markers.
Adrienne hands me the picture I drew
of the people on our block.
It is in a frame.
Our block is different now.
Most of these people haven't come back.
My mother says some live in other states,
and some are in Heaven now.

Me, Adrienne, Tommy and Keesha
want to do something special for our neighbors,
so Adrienne and Keesha make a wreath of flowers
and we hang the picture and the flowers on my tree.
That way, if any of our neighbors ever come back
or if they can see us from Heaven,
they will know that we didn't forget about them.

Adrienne

A whole year has gone by
and a lot of things are different,
but some things are the same.
I've still got friends.
And today, I get to play.
It's sunny outside and me, Keesha,
Michael and Tommy are
playing hide-and-go-seek.
Granny says Katrina's the worst storm
that's come this way in a long time.
She says it'll take a while
for things to get back to how they used to be.
But today, we don't have to worry about that.
Today, no one has to go home early.
Today, we'll sit on Granny's porch
and eat po'boy sandwiches.
Today, we'll play till the sun goes down.
Today, the sky don't look gray at all.
Seems like the sun is gonna shine forever.

We're from New Orleans.
We're from a place where people are tough.
Tough because of the things they've been through,
the things they've seen.
We're from New Orleans,
a place where hurricanes happen.
But that's only the bad side.

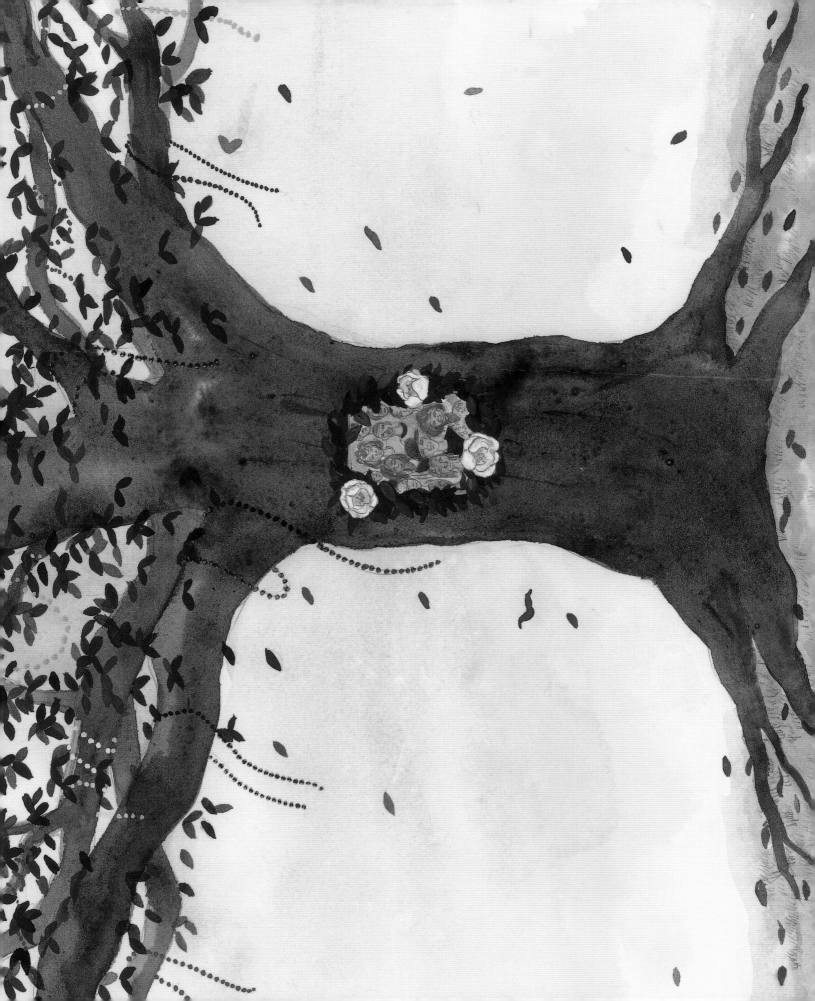

Theodore Mouse UP IN THE AIR

By Michaela Muntean

Illustrated by Lucinda McQueen

A Golden Book • New York
Western Publishing Company, Inc., Racine, Wisconsin 53404

One day, when the wind was wild and the sun was warm, Theodore Mouse washed his sheets and hung them out to dry. The wind caught the sheets and puffed them up like big, fat marshmallows, and that gave Theodore an idea.

"With a bed-sheet balloon," Theodore said, "I could fly!"

Theodore was always getting ideas like that.

"Restless," his mother would say.

"Careless," his father would say.

"What will become of him?" his aunts would ask his uncles.

But Theodore didn't care what anyone said. "Let every other mouse stay in his own little house. I want to see how other mice live. I want to see what other mice do. I want to see what they eat and how they play. I want to see the world!"

So, with his idea in his head and his sheet in his hand, Theodore climbed to the roof of his house. He strapped his knapsack on his back, and waited for a strong wind to blow.

His mother and father and sisters and brothers and aunts and uncles all ran out of their houses. They looked up at Theodore.

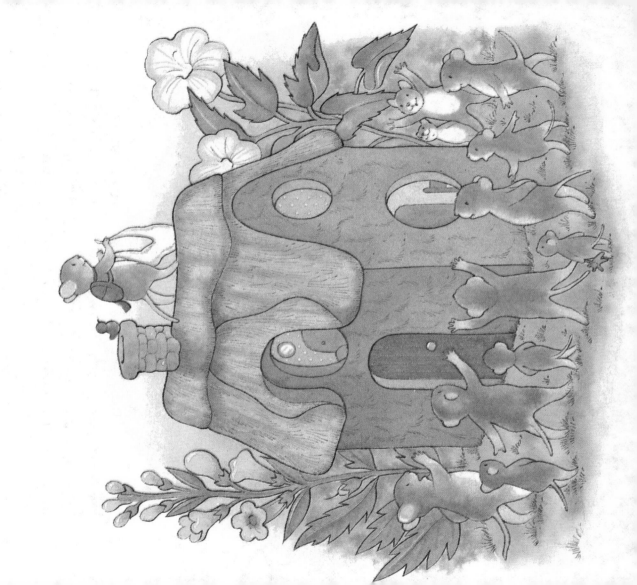

"You are not a bird," his mother cried.

"You are not a bee or a butterfly!" his sisters shouted.

"That's true," Theodore answered, "but I am going to fly. Watch me!"

"Be careful," his father called.

"Good-by!" Theodore cried, for there wasn't time to say anything else. His sheet caught a big gust of wind, and up, up, up in the air he went. Theodore Mouse was on his way to see the world!

Over the country he flew, riding the skies without a care in the world. Soon Theodore was looking down at a farm. From the sky, the fields and pastures looked like a beautiful patchwork quilt. Theodore would have liked to have a closer look at the cows and horses, but the wind hurried him on his way.

As Theodore flew, he found a way to go as high or as low as he wanted. He just had to swing his feet and raise or lower his arms. This was a very good thing to know, because Theodore was becoming a very tired little mouse.

As the sun began to set, Theodore swung his feet to the left and gently pulled on the right-hand side of his bed-sheet balloon. Down, down he drifted. Finally he landed on a rocky mountain ridge.

There was a group of mountain mice, all very surprised to see a mouse with a bed sheet fall from the sky. As they gathered around, Theodore told them of how he had flown there from his home.

There were many oohs and aahs, for not one of the mountain mice had ever flown. Not one of them had ever even left their mountain home.

"You must be hungry," a gray mouse said.

"And you must be thirsty," a white mouse said.

"Now that you mention it," said Theodore, "I am!"

"Then follow us," the mountain mice said.

They all helped Theodore carry his bed sheet up a
steep, narrow path. Over the ridge was a large clearing,
and around the clearing were many small, snuggly caves.
In the center of the clearing was a crackling campfire,
and over the fire hung a black pot full of bubbling stew.

A brown mouse handed Theodore a tin cup filled
with cool mountain spring water. Theodore drank every
drop. Then he and the mountain mice sat in a big circle
around the fire, and a fat gray mouse ladled stew into
little stone bowls.

Theodore had never tasted anything so good. "This is
delicious!" he cried.

After dinner, they each had a cup of tasty wild berry tea.

A full moon appeared in the sky, and Theodore thought the stars twinkled more brightly than he had ever seen them twinkle before.

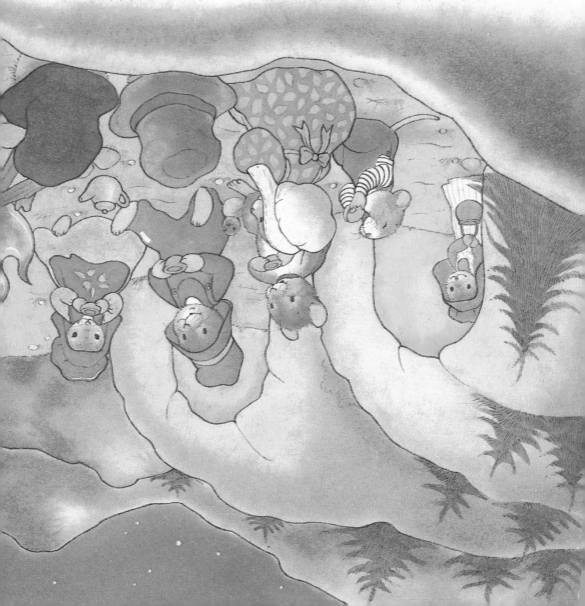

One of the mountain mice played a banjo, and another played a tiny silver harmonica. The other mice sang along with the music. It was a pretty song called "Rocky Caves," and Theodore listened very hard so that he would remember the words.

After they finished singing, a little brown-and-white mouse said it was time to tell stories. Then he told a scary story about a monster called Rattus who lived in a dark cave at the very top of the mountain. The story was so scary that it made Theodore shiver.

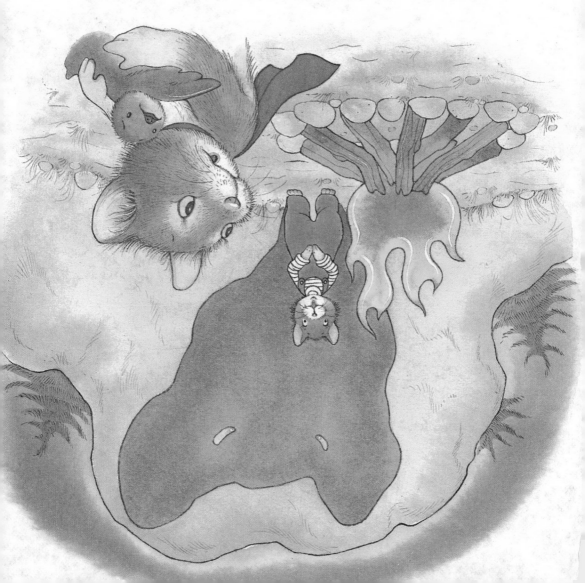

"I don't know any scary stories," Theodore said, "but I do know a funny one." He told them about the time his Aunt Winnie dropped a flowerpot on his Uncle Chester's head. "Everyone in the village took a turn at trying to pull it off!"

All the mountain mice laughed and laughed.

Now it was time for bed. The mountain mice gave
Theodore a sleeping bag, and they showed him how to
unroll it on a soft mat of pine needles. Theodore fell
asleep counting the stars.

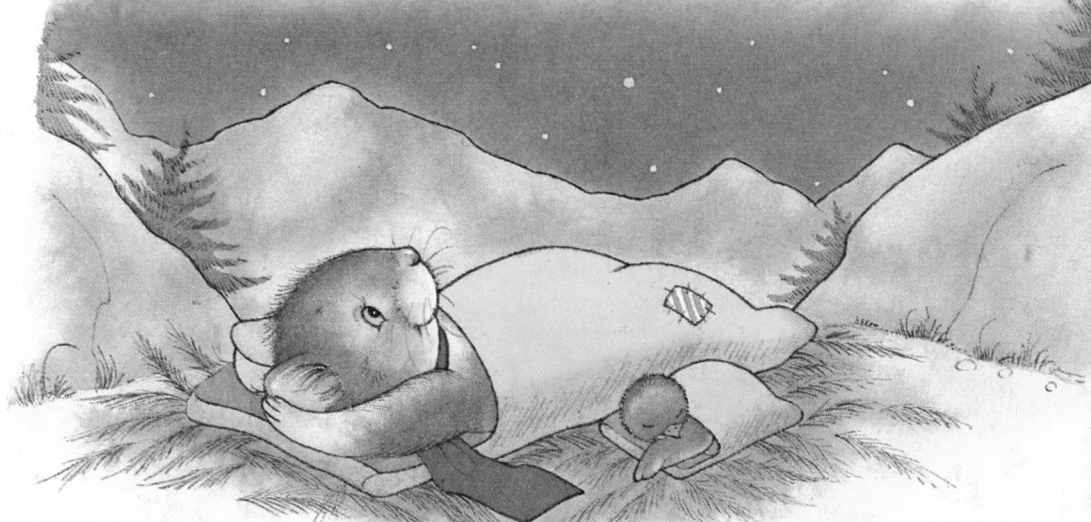

The next morning, everyone arose with the sun. They
ate delicious grain mush for breakfast, and then
Theodore helped the mountain mice with their chores.

The fat gray mouse wrote down the recipes for stew, and wild berry tea, and grain mush, and she handed them to Theodore. As a present, the other mountain mice gave Theodore a little homemade banjo. Theodore thanked them and put everything in his knapsack.

By noon, the wind was blowing hard, and it was time for Theodore to leave. All the mountain mice came to see him off, and they watched as the wind lifted Theodore up in the air.

"Good-by!" they called to Theodore. "Come back soon!"

"I will," Theodore shouted. "Thank you!" And then he was gone, sailing higher and higher, over the mountain ridge toward home.

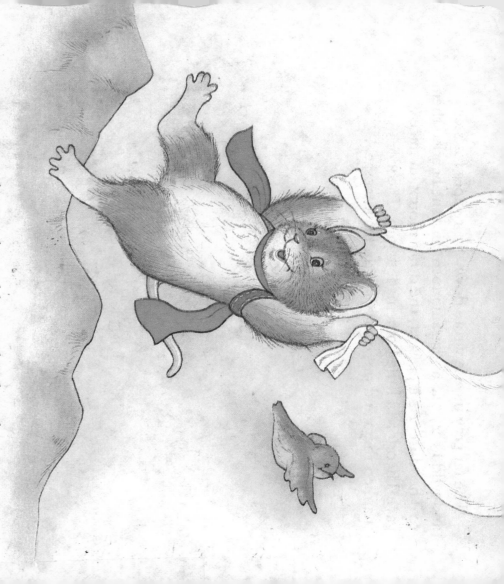